Special Reading

P^c

D1517375

SAILOR JACK

SAILOR JACK AND
    HOMER POTS

SAILOR JACK JACK AND EDDY

SAILOR JACK AND BLUEBELL

SAILOR JACK'S NEW FRIEND

SAILOR JACK AND
    BLUEBELL'S DIVE

SAILOR JACK AND
    THE TARGET SHIP

SAILOR JACK GOES NORTH

pictures by Marita Root

SAILOR JACK

AND

BLUEBELL'S DIVE

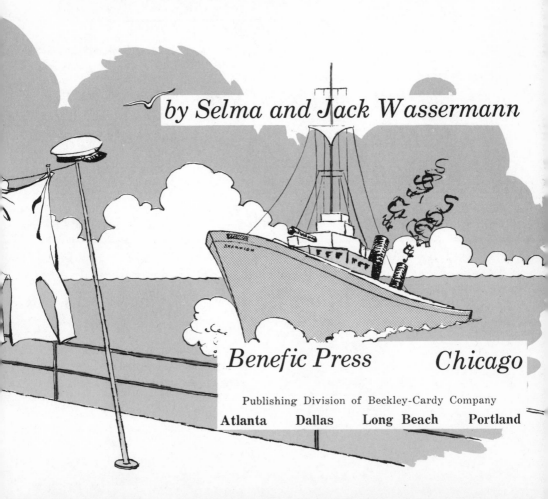

by Selma and Jack Wassermann

Benefic Press   Chicago

Publishing Division of Beckley-Cardy Company

Atlanta   Dallas   Long Beach   Portland

CONTENTS

Copyright 1961 by Benefic Press
All Rights Reserved
Printed in the United States of America

Bluebell
and the Sailors

This is the SHARK.
The SHARK can dive.

This is Bluebell.

Bluebell is not a sailor,

but she can work.

This is Bluebell
at work.

She works
with Sailor Jack.

7

Here Bluebell is not at work.
She is with the other sailors.
All the sailors of the SHARK
like Bluebell.

Here is Bluebell
with Captain White.
Captain White
likes Bluebell, too.

Bluebell can be in trouble, too.

Bluebell is in trouble, here.

Captain White called for all the men
of the SHARK to come.
They soon came.
Bluebell came, too.

"Men!" said the captain.

"You are here to see what troubles can come to the SHARK."

Bluebell did not like this.

"Aaaaaak!" she said. "Aaaaaak!"

The sailors laughed.

"Down, Bluebell!" said Jack.

"You will have to come down!"

Bluebell came down.

Then she and the sailors looked.

Captain White said,

"When we see this, we are

in trouble.

The SHARK must dive!"

"Dive! Dive!" said Bluebell.

"We must look out for this, too,"
said Captain White.

"The SHARK must dive!"

"Aaaaaak! Dive! Dive!"
said Bluebell.

"Here is more trouble,"
said Captain White.
"The SHARK will have to dive."

Bluebell jumped up.

"Aaaaaaak! Aaaaaaaak!"
said Bluebell.

"Dive! Ding! Ding! Dive!"

To New York

"That will be all, men,"
said the captain.

The sailors laughed at Bluebell.
"It is good to have you
on the SHARK!" they said.

The men all
went to work.

Jack and Bluebell
worked, too.

A call came
for the SHARK.
Jack went
to the captain.

"Look at this,
Captain," said Jack.
Captain White
looked at it.
"Here is something good, men,"
said the captain.
"The SHARK is going to New York.
Other ships will be there, too."

"We must all have on something
white when we are in New York,"
said Captain White.
"The SHARK and
her men must look
good then."

Bluebell looked at the men.
"Ding! Ding!" she said.
"We look good to Bluebell,"
said Jack.
The sailors laughed.

"Bluebell must
have something
new, too," said
a sailor.

Jack laughed.
"That is not
good for her,"
said Jack.

"I have it!"
said the sailor.
"This will be
good for Bluebell."

"Look at Bluebell!" Jack said.
The men looked.
Then they laughed.
Bluebell was in trouble.

Bluebell jumped.
"Aaaaak!" she said.
Down she came!

The sailors
laughed and laughed.
"Look! Bluebell
can not get up!"
they said.

"Here, Bluebell,"
said Jack.
"We will help you."

The men worked
on Bluebell.
"You must have
it on like this,"
they said.

"The SHARK will soon be in New York," said a sailor.

"Come on, Bluebell," said Jack.

"We will go up and see."

Bluebell's Dive

Jack and Bluebell looked.

All they saw was water.

"There it is!" said Jack.

Then they saw something more.

Soon the men of the SHARK
saw more of New York.
They saw other ships.
"Look at that big one!"
said one of the men.

All of the men came out
on the SHARK.

Captain White came, too.

"Are we all here?" he called.

"They must all see what a good
ship with good sailors looks like!"

On and on came the SHARK.
She came up to the big ship.
It was something to see.

Then the big ship did something.
It was something that said,
"What a good ship you are, SHARK!"

Bluebell did not like this.
She jumped up.
"Dive! Dive!" she said.
"Dive! Dive!"

The men down in the SHARK looked.
"That is the captain," they said.
"He wants us to dive!"
The men went to work fast.

They made the
SHARK dive.

Down went the SHARK!
"What is this!" said the men.

"Stop! Stop!"
called the captain.
"Stop this dive!"

The SHARK came to a stop.
But she was down in the water.

The men of the big ship
laughed and laughed.

"This is not something to
laugh at," said the sailors
on the SHARK.

But the men of the big ship
laughed and laughed.

"Not Good, Bluebell!"

Down in the SHARK no one laughed.
Captain White looked at the men.
He saw water, water, water.

Then Captain White looked
at Bluebell.

"That was not good, Bluebell,"
he said.

That was not good
at all."

"Aaaaaaaaak!"
said Bluebell.

Bluebell did not
like what Captain
White said.

She went to all
the sailors.

"Ding? Ding?"
she said.

The sailors did not
look at her.

Other sailors came.
Bluebell jumped here
and there for them.
No one looked.
No one laughed.

Bluebell went to work with Jack.
But Jack, too, did not look at her.

No one laughed at Bluebell.
No one looked at her.
Bluebell did not like this.
Up in the SHARK she went.

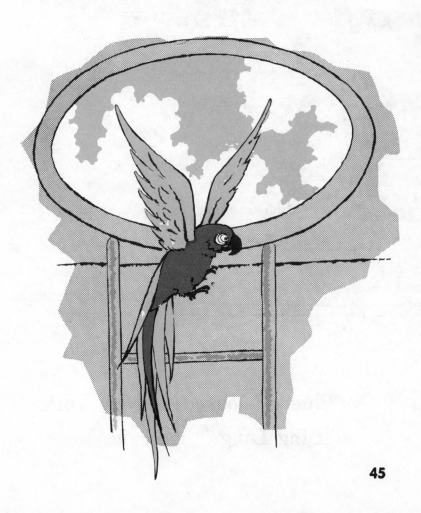

Bluebell looked at New York.
"Ding Ding?" she said.

But no one in New York
saw Bluebell.
And no one came.

The STARFISH

Down in the SHARK, Captain White
and the sailors worked.

Jack was at work, too.

"Here is something," he said.
"Captain White must see this!"

"This is not
good," said
Captain White.
"The STARFISH
is in trouble.
She cannot stop.
We will have
to look out
for her!"

Then Captain
White stopped.

"What is that?"
he said.

"It is something
up there, Captain,"
said Jack.

"I will go up
and see."

It was Bluebell.

She was jumping up and down.

"Dive! Dive! Aaaaaak! Dive!"
Bluebell said.

"You must stop that Bluebell,"
said Jack.

"You will have the SHARK
in more trouble."

But Bluebell did not stop.
"Dive! Dive!" she said.
"What is it?" Jack said.
Then Jack looked, too.

It was the STARFISH!

"Captain! Captain!"
Jack called.
"The STARFISH!
She is coming
at the SHARK!
She can not stop!"

"Dive! Dive!" said the Captain.

The men of the SHARK jumped up
and went to work.

Down went the SHARK!
On came the STARFISH!

Where Is Bluebell?

"All stop!" called Captain White.
"We will have no more trouble
with the STARFISH."

"But where is Bluebell?"

The sailors looked and looked.

"She is not on the SHARK,"
they said.

"Then the SHARK must go up,"
said Captain White.

"Bluebell must be in the water."

Up came the SHARK.

The men looked out at the water.

They looked for Bluebell.

But they did not see her.

The sailors looked and looked.
Then Jack saw something.
"There she is!" he called.
The men of the SHARK laughed.

Bluebell did not
laugh at all.

She did not look
at the men.

"What is it Bluebell?" Jack said.

"Trouble, trouble!" said Bluebell.

"Aaaaaaaak! Aaaaaaaak!"

"No, Bluebell," said Captain White.
"You are no trouble for the SHARK.
What you did was good!
It was good for the SHARK!"
Bluebell looked at the captain.
"Ding! Ding!" said Bluebell.
"Good SHARK! Good SHARK."

VOCABULARY

The total number of words in this book is 79, excluding proper names. Of these 42 are preprimer level. The 29 words shown below in roman type are primer words, and the 8 in italic type are above primer level. The numbers indicate the pages on which the words first appear.

all 8	laugh 13	soon 11
at 7		stop 38
	men 11	
be 10	*more* 16	that 18
but 6	must 14	them 43
		then 14
called 11	new 23	there 20
came 11	no 40	*trouble* 10
captain 12		
dive 5	of 8	us 36
	other 8	
get 26	out 15	was 25
going 20		water 29
	sailor 6	when 14
help 27	*ships* 20	white 21
her 21	something 20	work 6